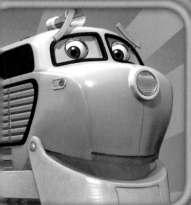

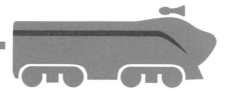

First published by Parragon in 2010

Parragon
Queen Street House
4 Queen Street
Bath BA1 1HE, UK

www.chuggington.com

ISBN 978-1-4075-6046-5

Printed in China

CHUGGINGTON™

Storybook Collection

Bath · New York · Singapore · Hong Kong · Cologne · Delhi · Melbourne

Contents

CLUNKY WILSON

Based on the episode "Clunky Wilson,"
written by Sarah Ball and Kate Fawkes.

One day, Chuggington trainees Wilson, Koko and Brewster, were ready to have a race.

Suddenly, they heard some horrible sounds coming from the repair shed.

CLUNK! CLANK! CLANG!

"What's that noise?" Wilson asked, his voice a bit wobbly. Koko dared him to go and look but Wilson wouldn't.

TOOT! TOOT!

"Chugger approaching," called Emery, a cheeky white train. "Hey, whatcha all doing?"

"Wilson's too scared to find out what the sounds from the repair shed are," teased Koko.

"Puffer Pete was inside there for a whole week once," Emery said. "They took all his wheels off!"

Wilson gasped. He never wanted to go to the repair shed.

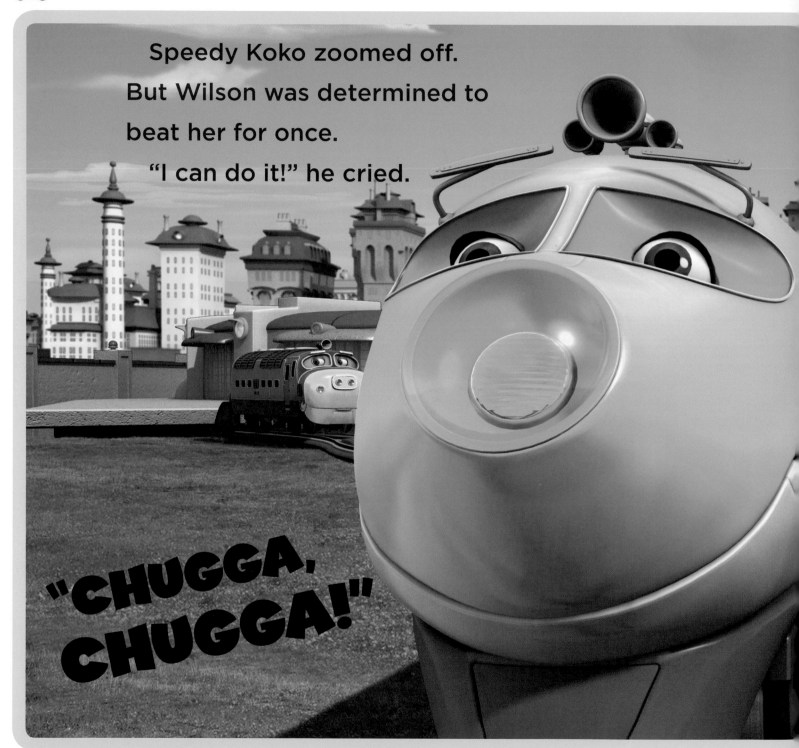

Speedy Koko zoomed off.
But Wilson was determined to
beat her for once.
"I can do it!" he cried.

"CHUGGA, CHUGGA!"

Meanwhile, poor Brewster began to puff – he just couldn't keep up with the others!

"CHOO, CHOO!"

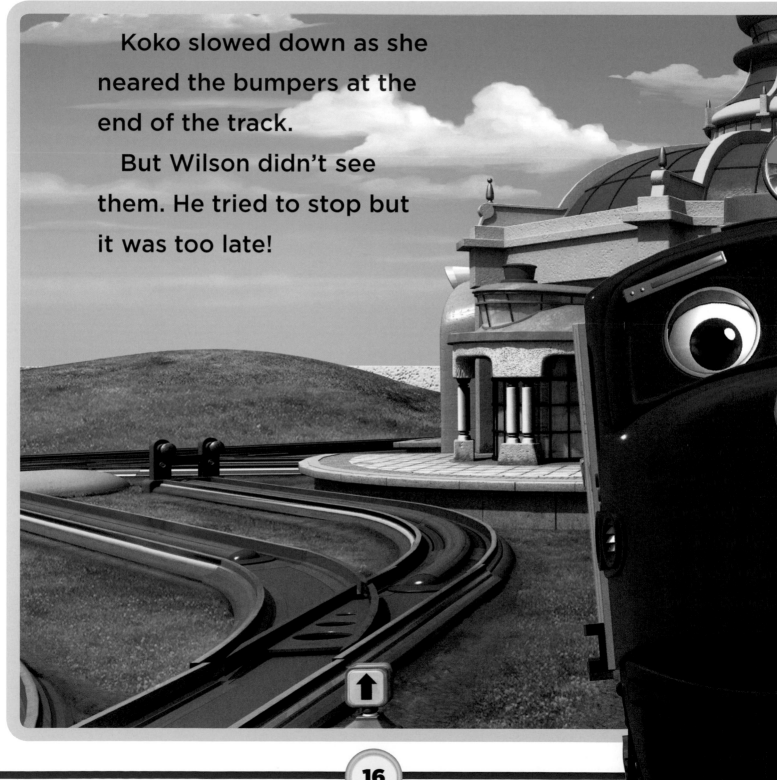

Koko slowed down as she
neared the bumpers at the
end of the track.

But Wilson didn't see
them. He tried to stop but
it was too late!

Wilson crashed into the bumpers. As he reversed, his wheels made a terrible noise. Something was wrong...

SCREEEEECH..... CRASH!

Just then, Vee made an announcement.

ATTENTION PLEASE.
WILSON, BREWSTER
AND KOKO TO THE
LOADING YARD!

"Wahay!" said Wilson, excitedly.

"It's training time!"

But as Wilson followed Koko and

Brewster to the depot, his wheels

made a scraping sound.

SCRAPE! SCRAPE!

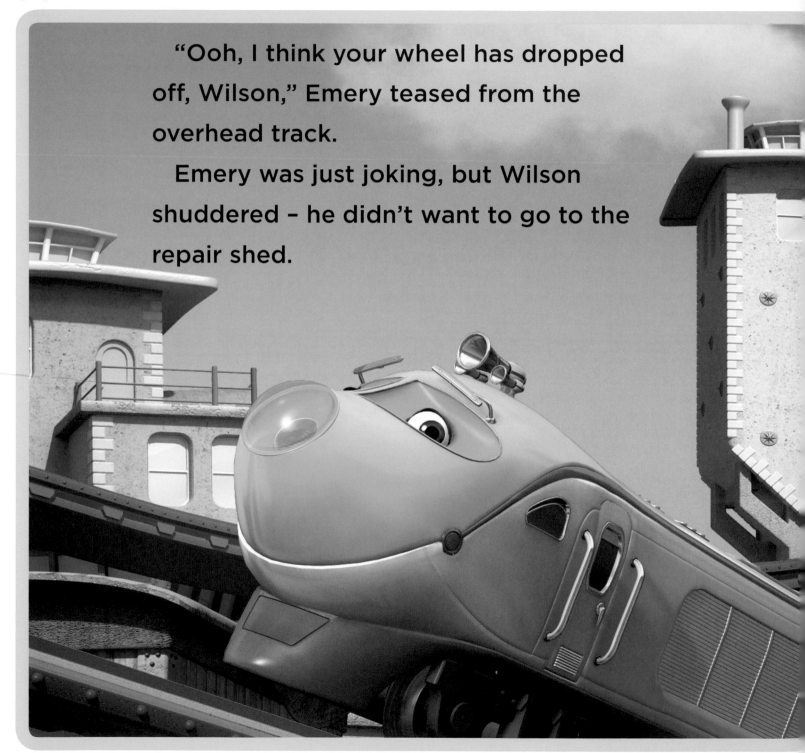

"Ooh, I think your wheel has dropped off, Wilson," Emery teased from the overhead track.

Emery was just joking, but Wilson shuddered – he didn't want to go to the repair shed.

In the loading yard, Wilson buckled up to a boxcar.
His wheels were still making funny noises.

CLUNKETY, CLUNK!

"What was that?" asked Dunbar.
"Sorry, got a little tickle in
my engine," said Wilson,
pretending to cough.

He knew Dunbar would send
him to the repair shed if he
thought something was
really wrong.

Vee sent the three trainee chuggers to take some things from the farm to the fair.

Koko loaded her boxcar with eggs, Brewster took some vegetables and Wilson got the cream.

Felix the farmer asked Wilson if he could ride with him to the fair too. He was hoping his cream would win a prize. But the journey was so bumpy...

...poor Felix spilled his carton of juice!

It was no good. Wilson couldn't ignore his problem any longer. He would have to go to the repair shed!

The red chugger shakily followed his friends back to the depot.

CLUNKETY, CLANK!

In the repair shed, Morgan the mechanic put Wilson on the rotator, so he could look underneath him.

"You're really brave," Morgan told Wilson.

"Most chuggers are nervous the first time they have to get fixed."

That made Wilson feel better. And soon, Morgan had mended Wilson's broken suspension spring. Wilson was as good as new!

Later that day, Vee called Wilson back to the fair to collect Felix.

Felix told Wilson that the bumpy ride shook the cream up so much that it was really thick. Wilson felt terrible.

"Instead, the judges thought it was the most delicious butter they had ever tasted," said Felix.

Wilson beamed with pride as Felix placed his first prize rosette on him.

"But next time there's something wrong with me, I'm going straight to the repair shed!"

CAN'T CATCH KOKO

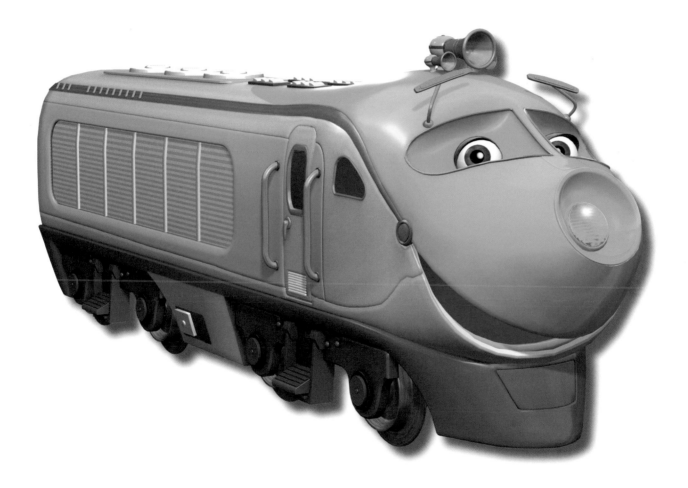

Based on the episode "Can't Catch Koko,"
written by Di Redmond and Sarah Ball.

One sunny morning, Chuggington's fastest train, Harrison, was in the repair shed. He had broken down the night before and needed a new part.

CLANK!

CLANK!

CLANK!

"I need to be fixed fast, Morgan, or I won't be able to make the delivery run tonight," Harrison told the mechanic.

Koko zoomed excitedly into the fuel yard. She couldn't wait to tell Wilson and Brewster about Harrison.

"Who's gonna do the night run if Morgan can't fix him in time?" asked Brewster.

ZOOOOM!

It would have to be someone really fast...

Suddenly, Koko's eyes lit up. She could do it!

Koko sped into the depot and backed up next to Dunbar.

"Oooh, please let me go, Dunbar," she begged. "I bet I can do the fastest run ever."

Koko had never done a night run before and Dunbar thought it would be a good experience.

"Traintastic!" cried Koko, excitedly. If only Wilson and Brewster weren't going too. Brewster was such a slow coach!

In a flash, the three chuggers were loaded up with goods and were ready to...

RIDE THE RAILS!

Vee made an announcement.

> NOW REMEMBER CHUGGERS, STAY TOGETHER.

But as soon as the tunnel light appeared, Koko shot off ahead of Wilson and Brewster.

"Bet you can't catch Koko!" she shouted, eager to make a speedy delivery.

At the other end of the tunnel, Wilson and Brewster caught up with Koko. The three friends gasped when they saw the beautiful, moonlit countryside around them.

TWIT-A WOO!

Wilson shuddered at the sound of the owl, but Koko whizzed on ahead.

"Betcha can't catch Koko!" she shouted.

Brewster and Wilson chugged after her. They had to stay together!

TWIT-A WOO!
TWIT-A WOO!

Koko rode down a side track and waited for Wilson and Brewster to appear.

"CHUGGA, CHUGGA! CHOO, CHOO!"

Koko could
hear their engines
getting closer.

A few moments later, Koko jumped out on them.

"**BOOOO!**"

she yelled, from the hidden track.

"You shouldn't do that Koko, I nearly fell off the track!" Brewster said, crossly.

"If you weren't so slow you would've seen me." Koko teased in a sing song voice.

"BREWSTER'S A SLOW COACH!"

But the chuggers didn't have time to mess around if they wanted to make the delivery on time. Koko raced off again, eager to impress Dunbar.

But then...

CREAK, CLUNK, SPLUTTER!

Koko's engine started to make a funny noise and she stopped moving.

"Wilson? Come back – don't leave me!" she pleaded.

But her friends had chugged ahead and were too far away to hear her.

Wilson and Brewster realised Koko was nowhere in sight. There were no lights on anywhere too – there must have been a power cut.

"Phew! Good job we're not electric then," said Brewster, feeling relieved.

Wilson and Brewster both gasped – but Koko was electric...

Meanwhile, Koko was feeling sad and lonely. Just then, she heard something in the distance...

It was Wilson and Brewster – they'd come back! Koko learned there was no power in the tracks to charge her engine. Now she was the slow coach.

"I'm sorry I teased you, Brewster," she said, quietly.

At the depot, Dunbar was worrying about the trainees.

Wilson suddenly came into sight, towing Koko behind him.

WOOOOOOO OOOOOOH WOOOOOOO OOOOOH!

cried Wilson, making a loud siren noise.

"Breakdown chugger coming through!"

"Brewster's doing the night run all on his own," Koko

told Dunbar.

At last, the power was back and Koko whizzed up and down the track excitedly.

Vee's voice rang out.

I'VE JUST HAD A MESSAGE AND YOU'LL BE PLEASED TO KNOW THAT BREWSTER'S DELIVERED EVERYTHING ON SCHEDULE.

"What a hero! Wahay!" cried Wilson and Koko, proud of their friend.

And Koko promised to never EVER call Brewster a slow coach again!

BRAKING BREWSTER

Based on the episode "Braking Brewster,"
written by Sarah Ball.

MORNING CHUGGERS.........

One morning, Vee had an exciting job for Brewster and Wilson.

"It's training time!" said Wilson, excitedly.

Brewster hoped they would be back in time to practise his new moves.

In the loading yard, Dunbar gave Brewster and Wilson hopper cars for training. He showed them what to do when they had a heavy load.

"Doors...drop load. Got it," said Brewster, confidently.

"DOORS... DROP... LOAD!"

Wilson found it really hard at first – but he kept trying.
Then he did it! **"WAHAY!"**

The two chuggers were ready to start their journey. Dunbar warned them that it was harder going downhill with a heavy load, so they must come back slowly. Wilson listened carefully, but Brewster whizzed ahead.

Vee told the chuggers to go to the mountain quarry to collect stone. They were to take the left tunnel at the mountain.

On the platform next to them, Morgan the mechanic suddenly slipped over on some oil. Wilson watched as Morgan sprinkled sand over the oil so his feet could grip.

"WHOOPS!"

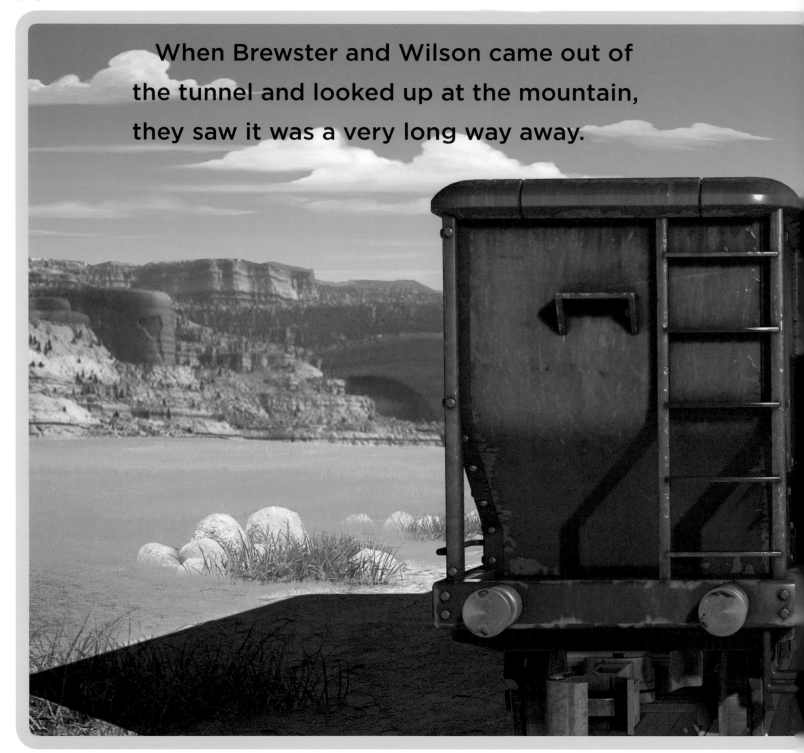

When Brewster and Wilson came out of the tunnel and looked up at the mountain, they saw it was a very long way away.

They climbed the track, higher and higher up the mountain. Suddenly there were two tunnels in front of them.

Wilson couldn't remember what tunnel they had to take. He wished he'd listened more carefully to Vee, but he thought they needed the right one...

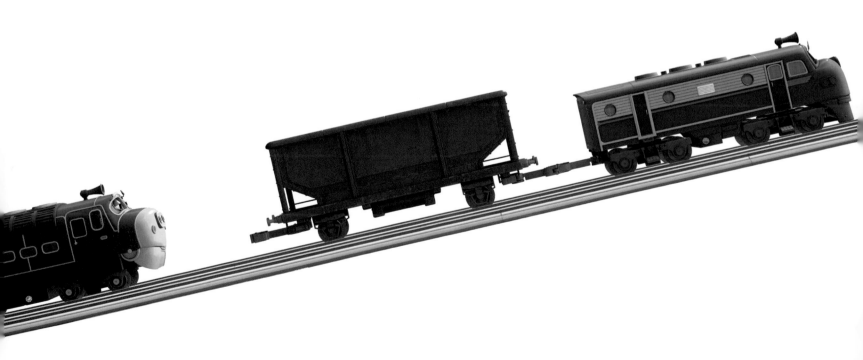

Before long, the tracks began to slope downwards.

"Honking horns – we're going downhill!" said Brewster, worriedly.

They were going the wrong way! After turning around, they rushed back uphill and chose the tunnel on the left this time.

When they finally arrived, Karen, the quarry worker, loaded stones into Wilson's hopper car. Wilson struggled to keep his doors shut so Brewster offered to go first.

But when it was Wilson's turn, there was only dust left!

Brewster wanted to get back to the yard and zoomed ahead, but Wilson remembered Dunbar's warning – to be extra careful going downhill.

"Downhill's easy peasy," Brewster said.

Suddenly, the track became very steep and Brewster whizzed down the mountainside, out of control!

"My brakes don't work. Help! I can't grip the rails!" he cried.

As Wilson caught up with Brewster, he had an idea. He whizzed ahead of Brewster and dropped his load of stone dust on the track.

"Brake on the dust!" Wilson called. It worked! They both slowed down and came to a stop.

"Thanks, Wilson, you saved me," said Brewster, very relieved. Wilson had remembered that Morgan used the sand to help grip when he slipped on the oil.

The two chuggers made their way back to the depot. Vee was pleased to see them.

GOOD WORK, TRAINEES, AND THERE'S STILL PLENTY OF TIME LEFT FOR YOU TO PRACTISE, BREWSTER.

But Brewster had tried out enough new moves for one day.

"Now I know...if you're going downhill, you have to go..." Brewster said, pausing.

"SLOW! HA HA!" giggled Wilson and Brewster.

WAKE UP WILSON!

Based on the episode "Wake up Wilson!"
written by Ian Carney.

One evening, Wilson and Koko were chasing each other around the park.

"Can't catch me!" shouted Wilson, laughing.

"Here I come, slow coach," Koko replied, zooming after him.

YOU NEED AN EARLY NIGHT, WILSON. YOU HAVE YOUR FIRST MAIL RUN TOMORROW.

Vee said it was time for the trainees to go to bed. But Wilson wanted to have fun with Koko – he had forgotten all about the mail run!

At the roundhouses, Koko and Wilson dared each other to stay awake.

They lasted as long as they could, then Wilson heard Koko snoring.

"WAHAY, I WON,"

whispered Wilson, before falling asleep too.

ZZZZZZ

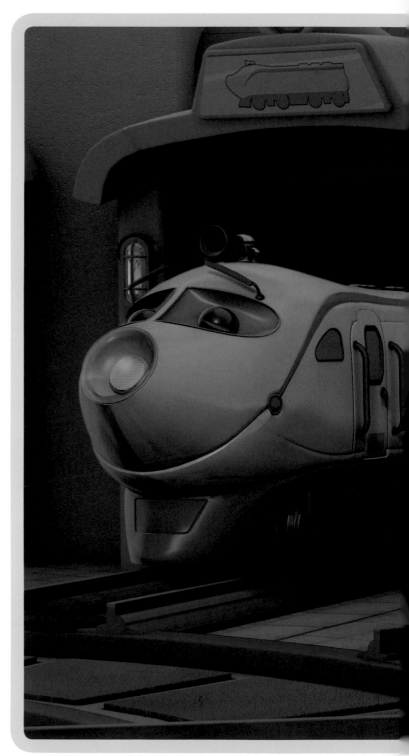

In the morning, Wilson chugged sleepily towards the rolling stock yard and coupled up to a mail car.

"You've practised with this mail car lots of times before," said Dunbar, and reminded him what to do.

YAWN!

By the time Wilson reached the second station stop, he felt really sleepy.

Eddie spotted Wilson from the track above.

"Watch out, Wilson, your door's open mate," he said.

Yawning, Wilson thanked Eddie and drove into the tunnel.

Wilson felt even sleepier inside the tunnel. It was dark and cosy, just like his roundhouse. He pulled over to the side of the track and fell asleep.

Meanwhile, Vee was looking for Wilson. He was supposed to be at the sorting office by noon.

WILSON, WHERE ARE YOU?....

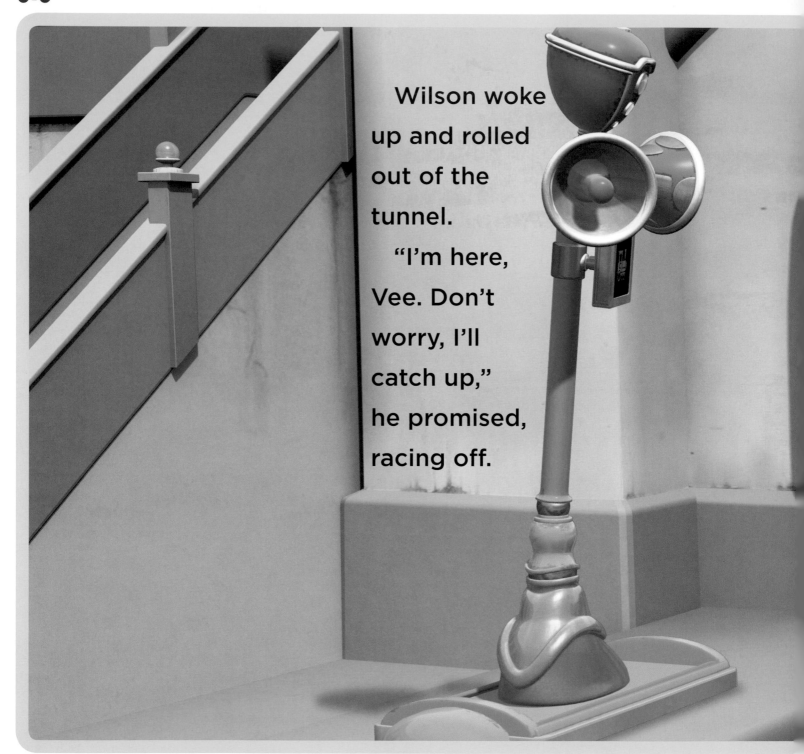

Wilson woke up and rolled out of the tunnel.

"I'm here, Vee. Don't worry, I'll catch up," he promised, racing off.

Back at the depot, Koko overheard Dunbar and Vee talking about Wilson. They were worried he wouldn't make it to the sorting office on time.

"Oh, no! Wilson's tired 'cause I kept him up so late," thought Koko.

She raced off to see if she could help her sleepy friend.

"CHOO CHOO!"

Koko soon found Wilson who was asleep again at the side of the track.

"Wake up, Wilson!" cried Koko, sounding her horn.

HONK

Wilson woke up and gasped.

"Oh no! I've gotta shift my gears!"

HONK!

At last, Wilson reached the sorting office with the Chuggington post. But the rest of the mail had already been taken to the branch stations.

"The Chuggington post has never been late before," said the postmistress.

Wilson felt terrible. It was all his fault.

Suddenly, he had an idea... he could sort the mail now and take it to all the branch stations himself. It would take a long time but the postmistress agreed to give it a try.

The mail was sorted into sacks, before being loaded into Wilson's car. Then Wilson dropped off a sack at each station.

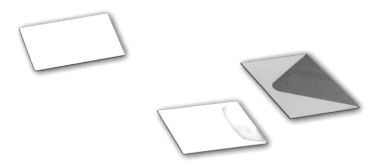

At last, Wilson chugged into the depot. He'd done it! He had delivered all the Chuggington mail.

"I'm sorry I let you all down. It won't happen again," Wilson promised.

And it didn't! That night, Wilson had lots of sleep, and the next morning, he did the mail run on time.

KOKO AND THE TUNNEL

Based on the episode "Koko and the Tunnel,"
written by Sarah Ball.

One day, as the trainees were heading to the training yard, they saw a tunnel they hadn't noticed before. It went underground!

Koko was really excited and wanted to explore, but Vee reminded her that there were important things to learn before trains could go down tunnels by themselves.

At the training yard, Dunbar was teaching the chuggers how to switch tracks.

"Once you leave the depot, you have to change the tracks yourselves," he said. "The arrow shows you which way it goes."

"I bet it's easy to do," replied Koko, confident she could do it.

But none of the trainees could get the tracks to switch.

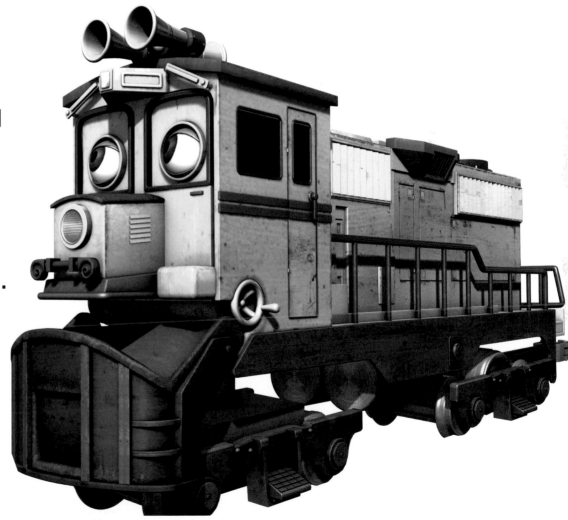

Before Dunbar
could show them
how to control the
tracks he was called
away by Vee.

"Let's work
out how to do it
ourselves!" Brewster
suggested.

So Brewster and Wilson tried all the different ways they could think to switch the tracks.

Koko started to get bored as she watched her friends struggle.

"This is riveting," she said.

"I'm going to explore the tunnel instead! It will be a real adventure." Koko said.

"Honking horns!" Brewster replied, refusing to go.

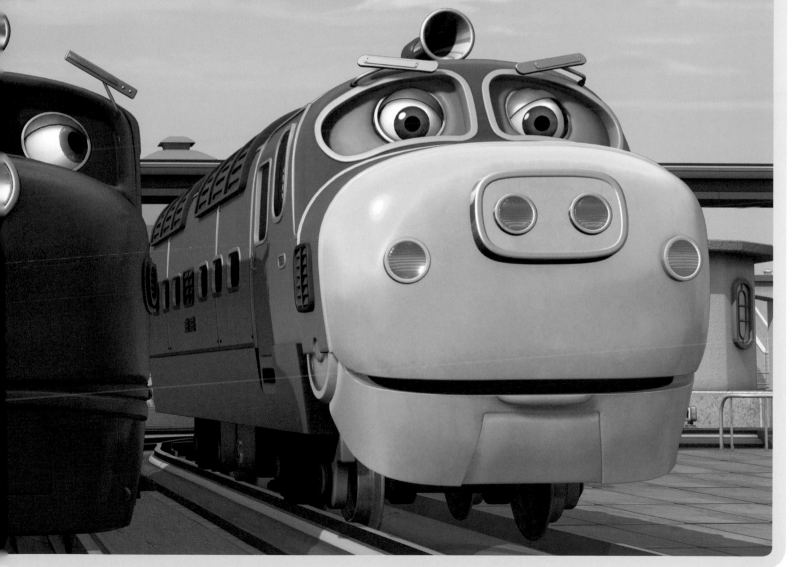

"Scaredy chugger!" teased Koko as she rode away with Wilson. "Don't tell anyone where we have gone."

"You'll get in carloads of trouble!" Brewster called, worried about his friends.

Inside the tunnel, Wilson started to feel uneasy.

"Maybe we should go back," he suggested.

"No way! We need to see what's on the other side!" Koko said as she went further into the tunnel.

"CHOO, CHOO!"

The two friends emerged into bright countryside.

"Wow! We must have come a really long way! But let's go back now, Koko." Wilson said, nervously.

"Ok, we'll find somewhere to turn soon," Koko called as she raced ahead.

"I want to go home..." Wilson whined as he followed her further down the track.

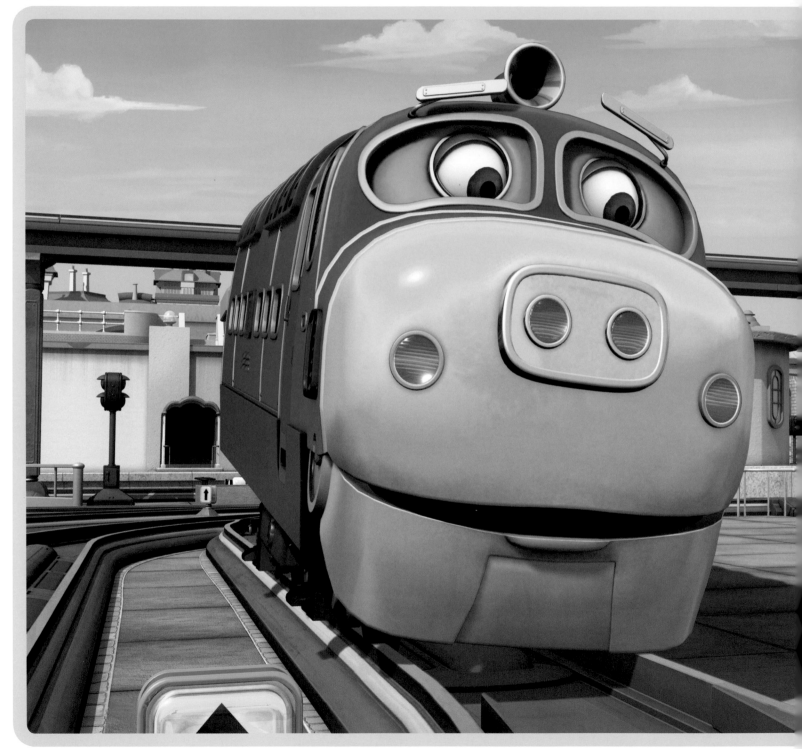

Brewster continued to practise at the training yard, trying to get the track to switch, but it wasn't working.

"Honking horns, this is hard," he said to Peckham the dog.

Out in the countryside, Koko came to a loop in the track, but the junction was set to straight ahead. She couldn't switch the tracks! Koko drove fast towards the track, but it wouldn't budge.

"Oh, bumpers!" Wilson sighed.

Koko tried again, speeding towards the turn.

"Wait Koko," Wilson called, but it was too late! With a loud crunch and a clatter, she zoomed off the rails and landed on the ground.

"Oh, no, I can't move," Koko moaned.

At the depot, Brewster was really starting to worry and decided to talk to Vee.

"Can you ask Calley to help please?"

OF COURSE, BREWSTER.

After a long search, Calley found the trainees and winched Koko onto the track.

"From now on, I'm not going anywhere until I know how to be safe on the rails!" Koko said.

"THANKS, CALLEY!"

"It really wasn't very sensible to go off like that," Brewster said to his friends when they were getting ready for sleep.

"I know. I'm sorry that I made you so worried. I'm lucky to have a traintastic friend like you," Koko smiled.

BREWSTER GOES BANANAS

Based on the episode "Brewster Goes Bananas,"
written by Simon Jowett.

One morning, Dunbar was teaching the trainees how to pick up sacks of post without stopping. "That's so cool," Brewster said. He couldn't wait to start practising!

But before he could start, Vee needed Brewster to do a job.

"Sorry to take you away from your training, Brewster, but some bananas need to go to the safari park urgently," she said.

Peckham the dog wanted to go too! He jumped in Brewster's carriage and they sped away towards the safari park.

Meanwhile, Wilson was practising picking up the mail sack. He missed the sack the first time he tried, but Dunbar showed him how to do it again. It was so much fun!

"DOOR OPEN... NET OUT... SCOOP!"

At the safari park, Mtambo told Brewster something strange as the boxes were unloaded.

"All the bananas went missing in the middle of the night!" he said.

"Bananas can't just get up and walk away!" gasped Brewster. As they talked, a monkey jumped across the roof and hid in Brewster's boxcar.

As they were chugging back to the depot, Brewster and Peckham kept hearing strange banging noises.

Peckham felt something tug his ear and looked around in confusion. There wasn't anybody there!

Then a banana skin landed on Peckham's head! He shook it off and barked angrily.

"Shhh, Peckham," Brewster said, worried about the banging noise that had started again.

"I better get Morgan to take a look," he said as they approached the depot.

At the training yard, it was Koko's turn
to practise picking up the mail sack.
"That was easy!" she said, smiling.

"Shall we go to see what happens to the mail at the sorting office?" Dunbar asked the chuggers.

"Wahay! Let's ride the rails!" Wilson called, and they rode away.

"I'm sorry, Brewster, I can't find anything wrong," Morgan told the chugger when he examined the boxcar.

"Are you sure it wasn't these bananas rattling about?"

There were so many bananas, Morgan picked one up instead of the phone by mistake!

"No, it was louder than that," Brewster said, wondering what the problem could be.

As he was leaving, the banging started again, so Brewster left the noisy boxcar at the shed with Morgan.

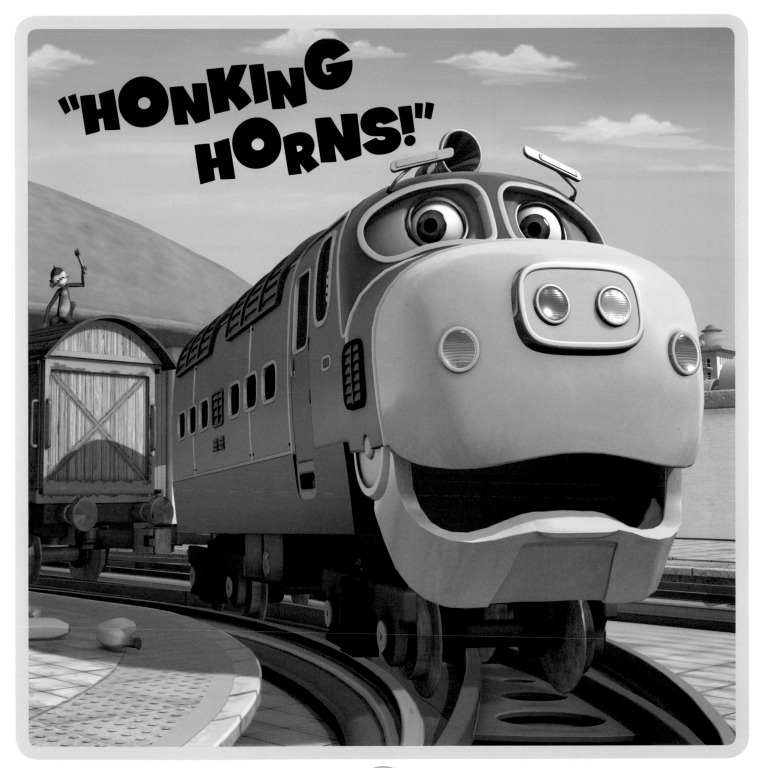

"HONKING HORNS!"

Brewster went to the empty training yard and practised picking up the mail sack by himself.

"DOOR OPEN...NET OUT...SCOOP!"

Just when he was about to scoop, the bag disappeared!

Funny things were happening to Old Puffer Pete too. As Lori was polishing his fenders, a banana skin flew through the air and landed on top of his whistle!

"Wherever did that come from?" Lori laughed.

Suddenly, Brewster realised odd things had happened since the safari park. He asked Eddie to leave his lunch out and hide. Sure enough, a monkey appeared! Brewster quickly trapped it inside the mail car.

"How did you know it was a monkey?" Hodge asked as Eddie let their cheeky friend out.

"Who likes bananas best?" Brewster replied.
"MONKEYS!" They all laughed.